To Lynne and Peter, who were the originals A.B.
To my father, with love J.T.

First published in the United States 1989
by Dial Books for Young Readers
A Division of NAL Penguin Inc.
2 Park Avenue
New York, New York 10016

Published in Australia by Penguin Books Australia Ltd
Text copyright © 1988 by Allan Baillie
Pictures copyright © 1988 by Jane Tanner
All rights reserved
Printed in Hong Kong
First Edition
(c)
1 3 5 7 9 10 8 6 4 2

Library of Congress Cataloging in Publication Data
Baillie, Allan, 1943—   Drac and the Gremlin.
Summary: Playing in the backyard a young girl
pretending to be Drac, the Warrior Queen of Tirnol Two,
unites with a young boy pretending to be the Gremlin,
to save the White Wizard's planet from
the Terrible Tongued Dragon.
[1. Play—Fiction. 2. Imagination—Fiction.
3. Fantasy games—Fiction.] I. Tanner, Jane, ill.
II. Title.
PZ7.B156Dr 1989   [E]   88-20275
ISBN 0-8037-0628-6

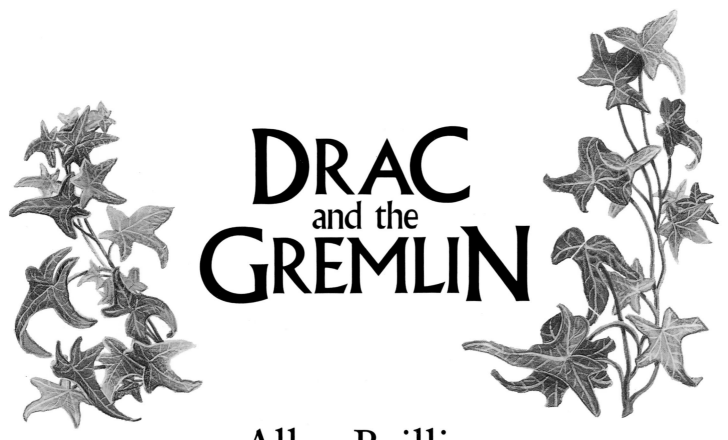

DRAC
and the
GREMLIN

Allan Baillie

pictures by
Jane Tanner

DIAL BOOKS FOR YOUNG READERS   NEW YORK

Shhh! Quiet . . .
Drac, the Warrior Queen of Tirnol Two, is in terrible danger.
She is fearless as an eagle, fast as a whirlwind, and wise as
the White Wizard.

Drac must capture the Gremlin of the Groaning Grotto.
He is quick and quiet as a panther, and twice as dangerous.
She must be *very* careful. . . .

"AAAARGH!"

Drac fights off the Gremlin's treacherous attack
with her ultra-laser beam.

She chases him into the quivering jungles, across the bubbling seas,
and through the dark, deadly fumes of the black volcano.

At last Drac traps the Gremlin in the misty valleys of Melachon.

At that moment
an emerald eaglon
slips from the sky,
bringing a fearful
message from the
mountain of
the White Wizard:

"Great Queen Drac, come to my aid before all is lost!
I am being attacked by General Min and her
hissing horde and you are the planet's only hope.
But beware the Terrible Tongued Dragon!"

Drac thinks for a second. Then she shakes the panting Gremlin:
"We must unite against this awful peril. You will join me
and we will save Tirnol Two!"
"GEDDOFF!" says the Gremlin, but he valiantly goes with her.

Drac and the Gremlin leap aboard her anti-gravity
solar-powered planet hopper. They sweep through the clouds
to the mountain of the White Wizard.

They land deep in the jungle and slither like
snakes toward General Min.
"Shhh. . . ." breathes Drac. "We will ambush her."
"Shuddup!" whispers the Gremlin.
They have arrived just in time. The White Wizard has
transformed herself into a silver flutterwing and is
trying to escape. But General Min is not fooled.
She is about to pounce.

"GOTCHA!"
Drac and the Gremlin spring before General Min can attack.

The General is caught by surprise.
With a howl of despair she flees deep into the jungle.

But the White Wizard hovers near Drac and whispers softly,
"There is still more danger! More danger . . ."
Drac hears the trees of the jungle shaking behind her.

The Terrible Tongued Dragon is upon them!

Drac speeds through the jungle, but she
can feel the fire from the Dragon's mouth.
She turns to fight.
But the Dragon is too big, too fierce.
The terrible tongue is poised to destroy her.

But all is not lost.
The Gremlin mounts his supersonic jetbike and roars
to the rescue with micron-blasters blazing.

"Get him!" says Drac.
"BARRRROOOOOMM!" says the Gremlin fiercely.

Together they drive the Terrible Tongued Dragon from the mountain.

Later they return to the palace.
"You have saved the planet," says the White Wizard.
"We are very grateful. Please accept as your reward our highest honor, the Twin Crimson Cones of Tirnol Two."

Drac the Warrior Queen and the crafty Gremlin leave the palace
of the White Wizard for their secret jungle hideout . . .

always on the lookout for their next perilous mission.